LIBRARY LIL

by SUZANNE WILLIAMS

illustrated by STEVEN KELLOGG

Dial Books for Young Readers New York

For Mom and Dad,
who encouraged in me a love of reading and books.
—S. W.

For all those heroic librarians I have met in my travels.
With appreciation and warmest wishes.
—S. K.

Published by Dial Books for Young Readers
A member of Penguin Putnam Inc.
375 Hudson Street
New York, New York 10014

Text copyright © 1997 by Suzanne Williams
Pictures copyright © 1997 by Steven Kellogg
All rights reserved
Typography by Amelia Lau Carling
Printed in the U. S. A. on acid-free paper
First Edition
1 3 5 7 9 10 8 6 4 2

Library of Congress Cataloging in Publication Data
Williams, Suzanne.
Library Lil / by Suzanne Williams; pictures by Steven Kellogg—1st ed.
p.   cm.
Summary: A formidable librarian makes readers not only
out of the once resistant residents of her small town, but out
of a tough-talking, television-watching motorcycle gang as well.
ISBN 0-8037-1698-2 (trade)—ISBN 0-8037-1699-0 (lib. bdg.)
[1. Librarians—Fiction. 2. Books and reading—Fiction.
3. Reading—Fiction. 4. Tall tales.]
I. Kellogg, Steven, ill. II. Title.
[PZ7.W66824Li 1997] [E]—dc20 95-23490 CIP AC

The full-color artwork was prepared using ink and pencil line
and watercolor washes.

I bet you think all librarians are mousy little old ladies. Hair rolled up in a bun. Beady eyes peering out at you over the tops of those funny half-glasses. An index finger permanently attached to lips mouthing "Shhh."

Bet you never heard about Library Lil.

Lil wasn't always a librarian, of course. She was a kid first, just like most people.

Lil in the tub. One year old.

Lil and Secondhand Rose. Three years old.

Lil on the soccer field. Five years old.

Lil builds Fort Rose. Seven years old.

And like most kids, Lil had a wild imagination. She loved to read, and she imagined herself the hero of every book she checked out of the library. By the time she was eight, she'd read all the books in the children's room.

Yes, Lil was a fast reader. And she had the most powerful, strong arms too. When the third grade soccer ball got stuck under the principal's car, Lil retrieved it.

Her strength might have come from carrying all those books around, for when Lil ran out of children's books, she started in on encyclopedias.

She used to check out a whole set at once. She'd walk down the street reading the "A" volume, held open in one hand, while she balanced the remaining volumes on the palm of the other hand. She turned pages with her teeth.

So it was no surprise to anyone when Lil grew up and became a librarian, landing a job in the nearby town of Chesterville. The townspeople soon dubbed her Library Lil.

Lil's specialty was storytelling, but when she advertised a storytime in the local newspaper, no one showed up. And when she posted a list of the fantastic new books she had ordered, no one came to check them out.

It was clear that the people of Chesterville were not avid readers. Television was their favorite form of entertainment, and Lil did not approve of TV. "Devil's Invention," she called it. "Keeps folks away from good books."

To Lil's way of thinking, TV was an evil that ranked right up there with poison ivy and mosquitoes. She knew she had her work cut out for her.

One horrible, stormy night the wind blew down some power lines. The whole town of Chesterville was plunged into darkness. TVs popped off like flashbulbs.

This was the chance Lil had been waiting for.

She fought her way through the driving rain to the town's ancient bookmobile, battling eighty-mile-per-hour winds that threatened to carry her away like a feather in an updraft.

Unfortunately that old bookmobile had been sitting idle too long. Its battery was deader than a pickled herring. But did that stop Library Lil? No, sir! Up and down the streets of town she went, pushing that bookmobile ahead of her just like a baby carriage.

By the end of the night every man, woman, and child in Chesterville was reading a book by the flickering light of a candle. The power was out for two whole weeks, by which time the townspeople had solidly formed the habit of reading.

Suddenly folks were borrowing more books than they had in the entire fifty years since the library had been built. And there was standing room only for Lil's storytimes.

Not long after the storm, a motorcycle gang rode into town. The leader of the gang was Bust-'em-up Bill. He was a towering six foot seven, and when he took off his jacket to play pool, he revealed a skull-and-crossbones tattoo that would scare the wool off a sheep.

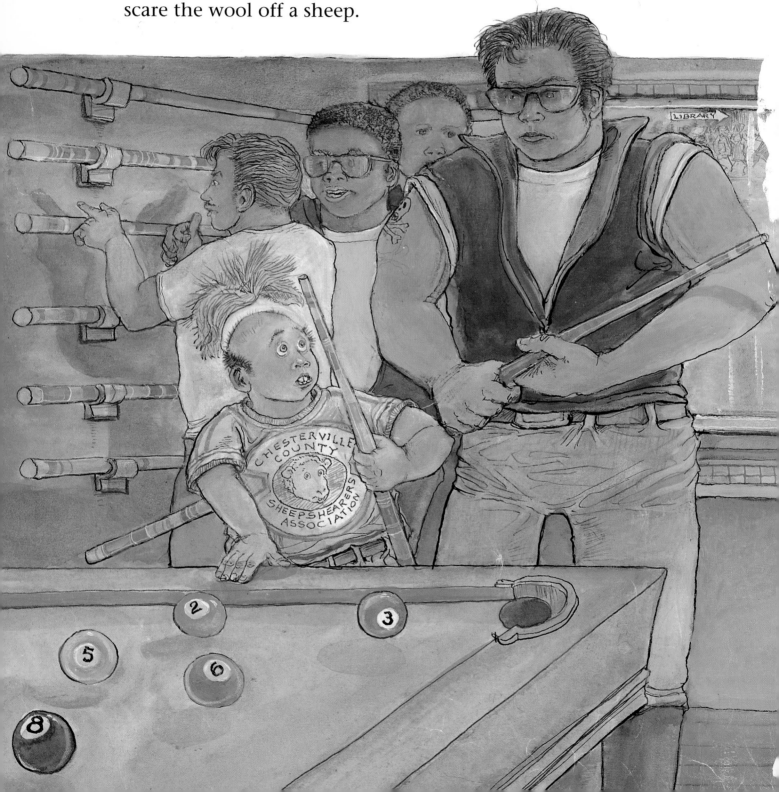

Now, at first Lil took no more notice of Bill and his gang than a duck would of rain. She was only interested in readers, and they kept her plenty busy at the library since the storm. So while Bill and his gang hustled pool at the local tavern, Library Lil checked out books.

It wasn't long before Bust-'em-up Bill found out about Lil, though. You see, he was in the habit of watching professional wrestling on Tuesday nights, so when Tuesday night rolled around, Bill expected to watch his favorite program.

"Where's the danged TV?" he yelled at the bartender.

"Don't have one, sir," said the bartender. "Nobody in town watches it much anymore. Too many good books to read."

"No one around here watches TV?" Bill roared. "What's the matter with you folks?"

The bartender chuckled nervously. "Lil's made us all into readers."

"Readers?" Bill laughed. It was not a pleasant sound. He faced his gang. "Did you hear that? These lily-livered cowards read *books*!" The way he said "books" left no doubt that to him, this was the filthiest word in the English language.

"WHO. IS. LIL?" He spat the words out like bullets.

"Our librarian," squeaked the bartender.

"Where is she?" growled Bill.

The bartender cringed. "She'll be parking her bookmobile across from the library in about ten minutes, sir."

Bill stomped toward the door. "Let's go," he grunted to his gang.

When Lil arrived, she found the parking lot filled with motorcycles and surly bikers. "Move your bikes," she called. "You're blocking my parking place."

"Tough cookies, sister," said Bill. "It's your fault I'm missing my favorite TV show."

"Listen," Lil said. "I don't want trouble. Just move the bikes."

The gang stood their ground.

"All right," said Lil. "If *you* won't move them, I guess I'll just have to move them *for* you."

"Did you hear that?" Bill shouted to his gang. "She'll move them for us. Sister, if you can do that, why I'll, I'll . . ." Bill glanced at the bookmobile. "I'll read a book," he finished. It was the worst thing he could think of.

Lil grinned. She flexed her skinny muscles. Then she stooped down, reaching under one of the motorcycles. Straightening, she suddenly hoisted the motorcycle with one hand and tossed it into the street. It cost her little more effort than flinging an apple core. Bust-'em-up Bill and his gang watched with their jaws hanging down as Lil threw motorcycle after motorcycle onto a stack reaching up toward the moon.

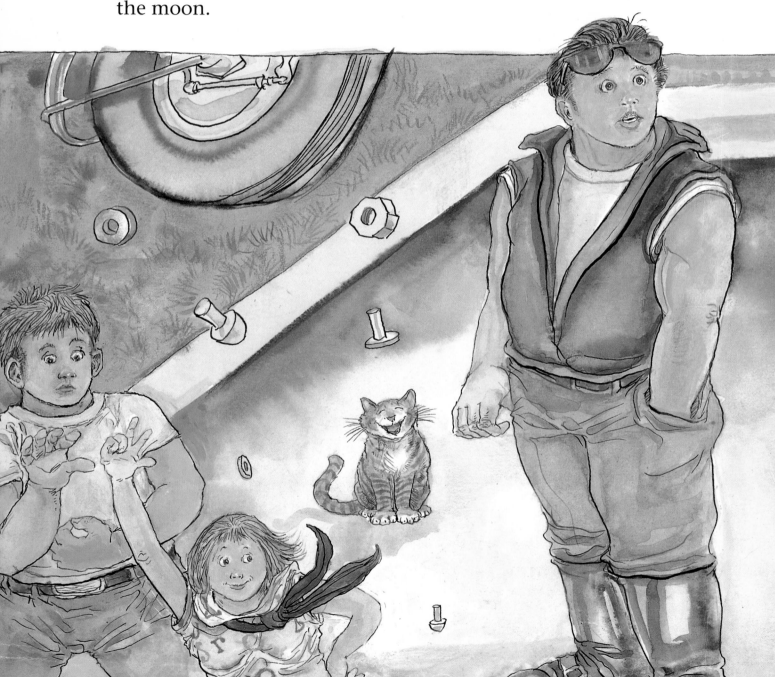

When she'd cleared the parking lot, Lil drove the book-mobile on in. Then she climbed down and headed toward the library's front door.

"All right, boys," she called out. "I'm open for business."

Bill's boys tried to sneak away, but Bill hauled them up by their collars. "Not so fast," he growled. "We're all getting books. If anyone tries to leave without one, he's gonna be reminded why my nickname is Bust-'em-up."

It wasn't long before every man in Bill's gang was reading away. 'Course some of them hadn't learned too well in school, so Lil gave 'em some easier books to begin on.

Several of the guys got into a fight over who was going to be the first to check out *The Mouse and the Motorcycle*.

Fortunately Lil found some extra copies and calmed things down.

Last time I was over to Chesterville, they'd added a new wing to the town library. Seems Lil's been busier than ever. She's had to take on a library assistant to help out.

The new assistant's a big fellow. The townspeople call him Bookworm Bill.

The kids think he's a whale of a storyteller, but then, he learned from a master.

Since Bill's been on the job, Lil says there hasn't been a single overdue book. *I* think she's kind of sweet on the guy. Says she's even taken to watching a little of the Devil's Invention—particularly on Tuesday nights.